How I Learn

A Kid's Guide to Learning Disability

For our nieces and nephews, who learn with joy and wonder. – BSM & CAP

For Marilyn and Mark, who are my North and South. – JAH

Published by
MAGINATION PRESS
An Educational Publishing Foundation Book
American Psychological Association
750 First Street, NE
Washington, DC 20002

For more information about our books, including a complete catalog, please write to us, call 1-800-374-2721, or visit our website at www.apa.org/pubs/magination.

Printed by Lake Book Manufacturing, Inc., Melrose Park, IL

Book design and composition by Sandra Kimbell

Library of Congress Cataloging-in-Publication Data
Miles, Brenda.
How I learn : a kid's guide to learning disability /
by Brenda S. Miles, PhD, and Colleen A. Patterson, MA ;
illustrated by Jane Heinrichs.
pages cm
ISBN 978-1-4338-1660-4 (hardcover) — ISBN 1-4338-1660-1
(hardcover) — ISBN 978-1-4338-1661-1 (pbk.) — ISBN 1-4338-
1661-X (pbk.) 1. Learning disabilities—Juvenile literature.
2. Learning disabled children—Juvenile literature. I. Patterson,
Colleen A. II. Heinrichs, Jane, 1982– illustrator. III. Title. IV.
Title: Kid's guide to learning disability.
RJ496.L4M55 2015
618.92'85889—dc23
2013048303

Manufactured in the United States of America
First printing April 2014
10 9 8 7 6 5 4 3 2 1

How I Learn

A Kid's Guide to Learning Disability

by Brenda S. Miles, PhD, and
Colleen A. Patterson, MA

illustrated by Jane Heinrichs

Magination Press • Washington, DC
American Psychological Association

I like school, but sometimes I get confused.
That's because I learn in a different way.

But guess what? That's OK.

If you are looking at this book,
I bet you learn in a different way,
too. And that's OK.

I am good at many things,
like sports, helping my teacher, and playing
board games. I am r-e-a-l-l-y good at drawing!
And I am GREAT at making friends!

I bet you are good at
many things, too!
What are you good at?

But, like everyone, I have trouble with some things, and that's OK.

Reading is tough. I can see the letters but I can't remember the sounds. And when I try sounding out words, sometimes I don't understand what all the sentences mean.

I write interesting stories, but Carmen, a girl in my class, has trouble writing. She has LOTS of ideas but she can't put them all down on paper.

I love math because numbers make sense to me. But math is tough for Henry. He jumbles up the numbers and feels frustrated.

I bet some things are frustrating for you, too.

What do you find r-e-a-l-l-y hard to do?

There's a reason why some things are hard for me,
Carmen, Henry, and for you, too.

It's called a learning disability, or LD for short.
Some people call it a *learning difference.*

There are different kinds of LDs. Some kids have trouble reading, like me. Other kids have trouble writing, like Carmen. Some kids have trouble with math, like Henry. And that's OK.

Some people might think that we don't try
hard enough, but that's NOT true!

We work r-e-a-l-l-y hard at school and feel proud of everything we do! LD means we learn in a different way, and that's OK.

The great news is we can do smart things to help us learn. You can do smart things, too!

But we have to work hard to make sure we do them. I raise my hand and ask the teacher for help when I don't understand what I am reading. Sometimes I use a computer that reads to me.

I work with Ms. King, my extra help teacher, at school.
She helps kids who have learning disabilities.

My parents read books with me. When we read together, and I ask questions, I learn new words and understand the story better.

When Carmen is writing, she makes a list of her ideas. Then she puts her ideas into sentences and her parents write them down. She finishes her work faster and her stories are longer that way!

Henry and his family make math fun by counting and measuring in the kitchen. At school, he uses a calculator to un-jumble numbers on math sheets.

Note to Parents, Caregivers, and Professionals

When a child struggles in school, it is difficult to find the words to help. Trying to determine exactly where the challenges lie can be a long and difficult journey for parents, caregivers, professionals, and children struggling at school. Once a child is diagnosed with a learning disability, or deemed a student with exceptional learning needs, another journey begins. How do you explain learning problems to a child? And what strategies may support academic success?

How I Learn provides parents, caregivers, teachers, and mental health professionals with a simple explanation of why some children struggle in school. The story introduces the concept of a learning disability in concrete terms for younger students, emphasizing that they are capable of learning, but that they do so in a different way. The story also supports a personalized discussion, encouraging children directly to identify their own strengths and challenges. Feelings typically associated with learning problems and strategies to promote achievement are also addressed.

You can encourage an honest and accurate discussion of learning difficulties as you read through this book with your child. Emphasize that many children find school challenging. Explain, too, that children—no matter how young or old they are—can use smart strategies to help them learn. Here are more specific suggestions to guide your discussion.

What Are Your Strengths?:
Stop reading after the narrator asks, "What are you good at?" Ask your child to list three strengths. Do not focus only on schoolwork. Playing sports, making crafts, singing, or playing an instrument are valuable skills, as well. Discuss three of your own strengths and celebrate what you and your child do well!

What Are Your Challenges?:
Stop reading after the narrator asks, "What do you find r-e-a-l-l-y hard to do?" Explain that everyone has tasks that are challenging for them. Talk about two or three things that you find difficult to do. Maybe it's cooking dinner or talking in front of people in meetings. Ask your child what he or she finds tough to do. Again, it is not necessary to focus only on schoolwork. Maybe your child struggles to ride a bike or to keep toys and sports equipment organized. However, since the story discusses challenges in reading, writing, and math, encourage your child to comment on these areas, if appropriate. For example, you might say, "You find reading tough, too, sometimes, don't you?" or "See, other kids struggle to write their ideas down, too!"

You Are Smart; You Just Learn Differently!:
Pause after the narrator says, "We work r-e-a-l-l-y hard at school and feel proud of everything we do! LD means we learn in a different way, and that's OK." Students with learning disabilities are very sensitive to what they can and cannot do compared to peers. Even if you are encouraging, your child may have heard words like "dumb," "stupid," or "lazy," and may assume they are true. It is crucial to provide your child with an alternate—and more accurate—explanation for learning problems. Stress that your child always works hard and tries his or her best, so words like "lazy" are just not true. Explain to your child that he

or she is smart and *can* learn, but it may take longer to figure things out. Share a personal experience when things did not start out well, but you were able to accomplish your goal with some help and creative problem solving. Emphasize that focusing on a goal, staying positive, and coming up with strategies for learning will help to get tasks done.

Use Smart Strategies:
Reinforce that having a learning disability can make school challenging sometimes, but there is help. For example, for students with reading disabilities, assistive technology (e.g., computer programs) will "read" books out loud as students listen. Explain that children who use this technology are reading with their "ears" rather than with their eyes.

You can help your child by using strategies, too.

Reading Strategies: When reading with your child, be sensitive to your child's reading level. If words that appear frequently (e.g., *the, cat*) are easy for your child to recognize, ask him or her to read those words, while you help to sound out the more difficult ones. At natural breaks in the story, stop and ask your child, "What do you think will happen next?" This line of questioning may help your child begin to use context to support comprehension. If your child says something that doesn't seem to fit with the story, try not to correct the suggestion. Instead, propose another idea and then continue reading with, "Let's see what happens." In time, you might offer an inconsistent ending to see if your child will correct your prediction once he or she has developed a stronger sense of story structure. Ask your child to visualize the story as you read it—as if imagining scenes in a movie—to boost comprehension.

Writing Strategies: Many adults feel that if they write answers down for their child during writing exercises then their child is not learning. However, "scribing"—writing for your child as he or she dictates ideas—can be a helpful tool. It is important to keep children engaged in writing while understanding the difficulty they have with this process. For creative writing, support your child by brainstorming a topic. Once you have the big topic, start brainstorming smaller subtopics with your child. For example, if the topic is the local zoo, some subtopics might be: where the zoo is located, how many animals live there, and the kinds of animals visitors will see while walking through the park. Jot these smaller ideas down on index cards—using just a word or two—and have your child arrange the cards to determine the desired and most logical order. Then, ask your child to look at each card and dictate a sentence about each idea as you write it down. Together, check the capitalization and punctuation of each sentence once the story is complete. As children get older, dictation software on a computer can replace parent or teacher scribing.

Math Strategies: Reinforce math concepts and number sense by having fun. For example, together with your child, measure ingredients while baking, count out moves while playing board games, or play card games like Crazy Eights or Cribbage. These activities may help your child understand sequential counting; concepts like addition, subtraction, and fractions; and comparison words like *bigger, smaller, more,* or *less.*

Make a Plan:
After you finish the book, begin looking ahead. Make a plan with your child to try one or two strategies together the next time work is tough. Using the language of the book, emphasize that "it's okay" to learn differently and to ask for help.

Continue the Conversation:
Learning needs and challenges will change across grades. Remain open and flexible with your child as you explore new strategies for supporting academic achievement. Do not hesitate to speak with your child's teacher or school psychologist about additional strategies to support learning or to inquire about evidence-based programs shown to improve reading, writing, or math skills. If your child needs additional emotional support, it may be helpful to consult a licensed psychologist or other mental health professional.

About the Authors

Brenda S. Miles, PhD, is a clinical pediatric neuropsychologist who has worked in hospital, rehabilitation, and school settings. She is particularly interested in evidence-based interventions and brain plasticity in the remediation of learning challenges. Her first book for children, *Imagine a Rainbow: A Child's Guide for Soothing Pain,* was published by Magination Press in 2006.

Colleen A. Patterson, MA, is a psychologist who has worked in the field of school and clinical psychology for the past 20 years. She is an advocate for students with learning challenges within the educational system. *How I Learn: A Kid's Guide to Learning Disability* is her first book.

About the Illustrator

Jane Heinrichs studied illustration at Camberwell College of Arts in London, England. She loves drawing, reading, and huge chocolate sundaes. Her first book, *Magic at the Museum,* was short-listed for "Best-Illustrated Book" at the Manitoba Book Awards.

About Magination Press

Magination Press is an imprint of the American Psychological Association, the largest scientific and professional organization representing psychologists in the United States and the largest association of psychologists worldwide.